RED RIDING HOOD'S FAVOURITE FAIRY TALES

RED RIDING HOOD'S FAVOURITE FAIRY TALES

Dawn and Peter Cope

Royce
PUBLICATIONS

Acknowledgements

We would like to acknowledge the following
publishers who have granted us permission to
use their copyright material in this book:

A & C Black for permission to reproduce work
by Charles Folkard.

J Salmon for permission to reproduce work by
Flora White from their book **Favourite Fairy Tales**.

The Oxford University Press for permission to
reproduce work by Millicent Sowerby.

Every effort has been made to contact the true
copyright holders of work reproduced in this
book and in case of error or omission the copyright
holder is requested to contact Webb & Bower Limited.

First published in Great Britain in 1981 by
Webb & Bower (Publishers) Ltd

Designed by Cope and Davies Ltd

This edition published in 1983 by
Treasure Press
59 Grosvenor Street
London W1

© 1981 Webb & Bower (Publishers) Ltd

ISBN 0 907812 52 X

Printed in Hong Kong

Contents

Introduction

Fairy tales were handed down by constant repetition from generation to generation, their origins often blurred and indistinct through the passage of time. But their universal popularity was established by Charles Perrault (1628–1703), the Brothers Grimm (1785–1863 and 1786–1859) and others who collected and compiled the early fairy tale anthologies.

In this collection is included one story from another culture. *The Feather of Finist the Falcon* is a tale (or *skazki*) of Russian origin. It is a sample of a folk lore steeped in as much fantasy as our own, its origins going back to the very beginnings of the Slavonic race. The pictures by Ivan Bilibin are classics amongst Russian fairy tale illustration, and his striking drawings bear the characteristics of Russian art in the Middle Ages.

The Victorians particularly, liked mystical tales and the introduction of commercial colour printing during the middle of the nineteenth century served only to increase their appetite. More and more illustrators were thus given the chance to add to the stories rich and varied imagery. Ever since, the magic and fairy enchantment that they contain has never ceased to attract children of all ages the world over.

Such was their popularity that fairy tales were turned into the ever-popular Christmas pantomimes, used in toys, games and advertisements, as well as being printed on to fancy tins, greetings cards and colourful scraps.

The turn of the century brought with it a craze for picture postcards, when people not only sent millions of cards but amassed huge collections. Postcard publishers produced pictorial cards to suit all tastes, including all the favourite children's themes: nursery rhymes, games and pastimes, scenes from fairyland and many more.

It is interesting to note that almost all illustrators of children's postcards were women. Postcard illustration was never highly paid work and, for many, only provided a supplementary income. Women illustrators of popular books and annuals for children, water colourists, portraitists, miniaturists and

1903 advertisement for postcards. Cards from Series 37 can be seen on pages 46 and 49. An example from Series 31 is on page 30 of the companion volume to this book.

talented part-time illustrators working at home would have found children's postcards a natural choice. The famous illustrators of the day—Rackham, Dulac, Charles Robinson and the like, earned far more illustrating books.

While some of the illustrators were self-taught, many on completing their training at art school found picture postcards to be one of the first outlets for their work. Usually designs were submitted speculatively and, if accepted, publishers would pay (in the mid 1920s) around three guineas for a set of six finished illustrations. The more ambitious and successful went on to combine this with remunerative advertising commissions and children's book illustration.

Illustrating fairy tales on postcards presented artists with a particular problem. Generally, although not always, publishers and retailers preferred a set of six postcards to feature different stories. The artist had then to choose one scene which captured the atmosphere of the story to the full. When illustrating a book, on the other hand, the artist could draw perhaps half a dozen scenes depicting key events in the story.

Other children's classics, such as Lewis Carroll's *Alice in Wonderland* and

J. M. Barrie's *Peter Pan*, also provided popular themes for postcard artists as did familiar scenes from Dickens and Shakespeare.

The pictures in this book contrast in many ways. Some of the early designs are full of chilling Victorian drama, as the anonymous illustrations for 'Hansel and Gretel' on pages 18 and 20 show. They were beautifully printed in up to sixteen separate colours. Other early designs are crude by comparison but colourful and no less dramatic. It was not usual in the early years for postcard illustrators to sign their work, although later on it became normal practice.

Illustrators like Hilda Miller (1876–1939) were appealing to children of a different era, for fashions and attitudes had moved into the twentieth century. Her designs, drawn around 1920, for 'The Sleeping Beauty' and 'The Goose Girl' on pages 22 and 24 are characteristic of a style more delicate in its appeal, though less dramatic than earlier illustrations.

Hilda Miller

Millicent Sowerby (1878–1967) was one of the most prolific and popular illustrators of the 'twenties. Her characters were always gentle happy little people (some would describe them as fay), and they obviously appealed to the younger children. Her colourful designs, like 'Jack and the Beanstalk' on page 15 were to be seen regularly on postcards, playbooks and annuals of the period.

Introduction

Millicent Sowerby

The postcards selected here to illustrate 'Cinderella' emphasize the enormous stylistic variety in nursery postcard illustration. Compare the rather sombre picture of Cinderella sitting by the fireside in her rags, painted around 1900 by an anonymous artist, with later, more stylized designs of the ugly sisters by Folkard, and Cinderella at the ball in the Art Deco mode of Joyce Mercer.

Joyce Mercer

Joyce Mercer (1896–1965) spurned the popular style of her contemporaries, dismissing it as being too soft and sentimental. She preferred strong, bright, decorative design, filled with crisp detail.

Charles Folkard (1878–1963) was best known as a book illustrator. His illustration of Cinderella's ugly sisters on page 53 was one of a series commissioned by A & C Black for *Grimms' Fairy Tales* published in 1911. His bold, grotesque figures, formed with such confidence, belong to the world of Rackham and Dulac. (This is in complete contrast to his other claim to fame—Teddy Tail, The Mouse with the Eton collar, whom he created while working at the *Daily Mail*.)

Charles Folkard

Many a young child of a generation or so ago would have saved all the postcards he received and stored them in a big album, making for himself a wonderful book to dip into, and through which he could re-enter the fantasy world of the pictures and the stories.

Such richness of imagery found in fairy tales and nursery rhymes forms the basis from which children develop, and this volume gives us a rare chance to rediscover the world of fantasy enjoyed by children of earlier decades.

Popular children's illustrators of the twenties. Lilian Govey (1886–1974), Margaret Tarrant (1881–1959) and Susan Pearse (1878–1980).

Little Red Riding Hood

RED RIDING HOOD

Once upon a time there was a little girl whose grandmother made her a beautiful red cloak with a hood. The little girl loved it so much that she wore it all the time, and everyone called her Little Red Riding Hood.

One day her grandmother was ill and her mother said, 'Red Riding Hood, will you take this basket of cakes and goodies to your grandmother? She is very weak and they will do her good. Go straight there and do not stop to talk to anyone on the way.'

Red Riding Hood set off with the basket to her

Little Red Riding Hood

grandmother's cottage on the other side of the woods. On the way she stopped to pick a bunch of flowers and, wandering off the pathway, she met a wicked wolf who asked her where she was going. Red Riding Hood forgot her mother's warning and said, 'I am going to see my grandmother who lives in the cottage at the edge of the wood.'

When he heard this, the wolf thought, 'If I am cunning I can eat them both up,' and rushed off so that he could reach the cottage before her. He knocked on the door and a voice called out, 'Who is there?'

'It's Red Riding Hood,' said the wolf in a squeaky voice.

'Lift up the latch and come in my dear,' replied the grandmother, and in went the wolf and sprang on the old woman and ate her all up in a moment. Then he put on the grandmother's gown and night cap and made himself comfortable in the bed while he waited for Red Riding Hood to arrive.

Soon afterwards there was a knock at the door.

'Who is there?' called the wolf.

'It's Little Red Riding Hood,' she answered.

'Lift the latch and come in my dear,' said the wolf. 'I am too weak to get out of bed.'

Little Red Riding Hood came in with her basket of goodies. She thought her grandmother sounded strange but supposed it was because of her illness.

'Come here and take off your cloak, my dear', said the wicked wolf, 'and let me look at you.'

Red Riding Hood did so and then, looking more closely at her grandmother, she said 'Oh, grandmother, what big eyes you have.'

'All the better to see you with,' replied the wicked wolf.

'And grandmother, what big ears you have,' she said.

'All the better to hear you with,' replied the wicked wolf.

'And grandmother, what big teeth you have,' she said.

'All the better to eat you with,' cried the wicked wolf and sprang out of bed to catch Red Riding Hood and eat her all up.

The little girl screamed and ran to the door just in time to see a woodcutter passing by. He heard her screams and rushed to the rescue, killing the wolf with his big axe.

When Red Riding Hood told him that her grandmother

LITTLE·RED·RIDING·HOOD
RUNS·HOME·WHILE·THE
GOOD·WOODMAN·KILLS
THE·NAUGHTY·WOLF

PRESS·CARD·AT·BACK·THEN·BEND
AT·DOTTED·LINES·TO·STAND·UP

was nowhere to be found in the cottage, it occurred to the woodcutter that perhaps the wicked wolf had eaten the old lady and that she might still be saved. He took his knife and cut open the wolf, whereupon the grandmother jumped out, alive and well. She gave Little Red Riding Hood a great big hug, and thanked the woodcutter for saving their lives. They all sat down to feast upon the goodies Little Red Riding Hood had brought with her and, realizing how lucky she was to be alive, Red Riding Hood thought to herself, 'I will never again disobey my mother and wander off in the forest as long as I live.'

PUSS
IN
BOOTS

Once upon a time a poor miller died leaving all he had in the world to his three sons. To the eldest he left his mill, to the second he left his donkey and to the youngest he left his cat.

The youngest son complained bitterly. 'What use is this cat to me?' he asked. 'Even if I eat him and sell his skin, I have nothing else and will soon die of hunger.'

Hearing this the cat, not wishing to be eaten, said, 'Young master, do not despair. If you will get me a pair of boots and a drawstring bag I promise you I shall prove my worth.'

The young man obtained the boots and the bag for the cat

and gave them to him saying, 'Now I have not a penny left in the world. You must go out and prove yourself.'

Puss pulled on his boots, put some lettuce and parsley into the bag and sallied forth. When he reached a rabbit warren he placed the bag upon the ground and hid close by waiting for a rabbit to come and nibble the dainties within.

Before long a pair of plump young rabbits crept into the bag and the cunning cat quickly drew up the strings to trap them inside. Puss hastened to the palace where he asked to see the King. On being shown into the throne room he made a low bow and said, 'Sire, I have brought these plump young rabbits from the warren of my Lord Marquis of Carabas who commands me to present them to you with his respects.'

'Thank my Lord of Carabas', replied the King, 'and tell him that we accept his gift with pleasure.'

A few days later the cat trapped two fine partridges and these too he presented to the King with his master's compliments. In this manner the cat continued to present the King with gifts from his master, the Lord Marquis of Carabas.

On one of his visits, Puss learned that the King and his beautiful daughter intended to take a ride by the river the next day. That night he said to his master, 'If you will follow my advice your fortune will be made. Tomorrow morning go and bathe in the river just where I show you, and leave the rest to me!'

His young master did as he was asked and while he was bathing Puss took his clothes and hid them. Then, hearing the King's carriage approaching, he cried out as loud as he was able, 'Help! Help! My Lord Marquis of Carabas is drowning.'

The King put his head out of the carriage and, seeing the very cat who had brought him so many presents, he ordered his servants to go to the assistance of the young man.

While they were helping the Marquis out of the river Puss ran to the king and told him that while his master was bathing some thieves had run off with all his clothes. The King commanded his servant to fetch one of his best suits and present it to the young man.

When the young man was clothed, his Majesty invited him to take a ride in the royal carriage and he looked so fine and handsome that the Princess fell in love with him.

Puss, delighted to see how well his scheme was working, ran ahead of the carriage and said to the reapers in the fields, 'The King is coming and with him the Lord Marquis of Carabas. You must show your respect as they pass or it will be the worse for you.'

As the King's carriage approached, the reapers took off their hats and cried, 'Hurrah for the King! Hurrah for the Lord Marquis of Carabas,' and bowed low as they passed.

Puss ran ahead again and gave the same order to the reapers in the next field and the one after, and the King was most impressed by the young man's popularity.

As Puss ran on he came to a castle which belonged to the rich Ogre who owned all the land they had passed through. The cat knocked on the door and asked to pay his respects to the Ogre. The Ogre received him and asked him to be seated.

'I have been told', said Puss, 'that you have the power of changing yourself into any creature you wish.'

'That is true', roared the Ogre, 'and to prove it I will turn myself into a hungry lion.'

Immediately Puss found himself face to face with a hungry lion and had to admit that the Ogre was very clever indeed.

'However,' he went on, 'I find it difficult to believe that you could also turn yourself into something very small—say a rat or a mouse.'

At this the Ogre laughed a huge booming laugh and changed himself into a tiny mouse.

The instant Puss saw the mouse he pounced on him and devoured him.

In the meantime, the King's carriage had arrived at the gates of the magnificent castle. Puss went out to greet it saying, 'Welcome to the castle of my Lord Carabas.'

The King entered the great hall and wondered at the splendid manner in which the young man lived. A marvellous banquet was prepared for them and his Majesty was charmed by the good manners and noble fortune of the Lord Marquis of Carabas and was delighted when the young man asked for the Princess's hand in marriage.

They were married the following day and Puss was given the seat of honour at the wedding breakfast.

JACK · AND · THE · BEANSTALK
CLIMB, JACKY-BOY, UP TO THE SKY,
THE BIRDS AND THE CLOUDS GO A-SAILING BY.
CLIMB, CLIMB TO THE TOP OF THE STAIR,
WONDERFUL TREASURES ARE WAITING YOU THERE

Jack was the only son of a poor widow. He was an idle, good-for-nothing lad and although his old mother worked hard to keep them both fed and clothed, the day came when they had nothing left in the world but a cow. 'We have no money and no more food,' said the old widow, 'You must take the cow to market and sell her.'

So Jack set off with the cow, but on the way to market he met a butcher who offered him a handful of curious coloured beans in exchange for the animal. Jack was pleased to be able to sell the cow so quickly and hurried back home to his mother.

Jack and the Beanstalk

When the widow discovered that Jack had exchanged their cow for a handful of beans, she upbraided him angrily and threw the beans out of the window.

Next morning, Jack awoke to find large leaves shadowing his window. When he looked outside he discovered that the beans had taken root and sprung up to a great height. The immense stalks were thick and strong; they stretched upwards like a ladder until the top seemed to be lost in the clouds. Jack was curious to know where the beanstalk would lead. He climbed up and up until he reached the top and found himself in a strange barren land. Far away in the distance he could see a castle, so he started walking towards it, hoping to find food and shelter; he was tired and hungry after his long climb.

The castle door was opened by an ugly Giantess who took pity on Jack and invited him into her kitchen where she gave him food and drink. Then she said, 'You must hide, for my husband will return soon and if he finds you here, he will eat you for his supper.'

No sooner had she hidden Jack in a cupboard than she heard her husband coming. 'Fe-fi-fo-fum,' roared the Giant. 'I smell the blood of an Englishman!' But the Giantess assured him that it was only his supper cooking.

When he had satisfied his hunger with a huge supper, the Giant called for his magic hen, which, at his command and to Jack's amazement, laid eggs of solid gold. The Giant amused himself for some time with his hen and eventually fell asleep in front of the fire.

When he was quite sure the Giant was fast asleep, Jack crept out of his hiding place, seized the hen and ran off with her. He found his way back to the beanstalk and clambered down, still clutching the hen which he presented to his overjoyed mother. For some time, Jack and his mother lived happily; the hen produced as many golden eggs as they wished and they became very rich. But after a while, Jack became restless for he longed to climb the beanstalk and pay the Giant another visit in order to carry off more of his treasures.

A few days later, he rose early and climbed the beanstalk. When, at last, he reached the top, he was tired and hungry, but he set off for the castle as before and persuaded the Giantess to feed him and give him shelter for the night.

Once more the Giantess fed him well and then told him to hide in the cupboard before her husband returned home.

The Giant returned at his usual time and Jack heard him roar, 'Fe-fi-fo-fum, I smell the blood of an Englishman!'

Again, his wife assured him there was no one else in the kitchen, so he sat down to his supper. After he had eaten his fill, the Giant called for his bags of silver and gold and proceeded to empty them on to the table.

Jack was amazed to see the heaps of treasure and longed to have them for himself. When the Giant had counted it all up and tied the bags securely, he laid his head in his arms and slept, snoring very loudly.

As soon as Jack was sure the Giant was sound asleep, he stole out of his hiding place, grabbed the money bags and made off for home as fast as he could go.

Although Jack and his mother lived in luxury, he still wanted to return again to the castle at the top of the beanstalk.

So one fine day he climbed the beanstalk again and made his way to the castle. This time he had great difficulty in persuading the Giantess to allow him in, but at last she agreed and everything happened exactly as before. But this time, after he had eaten, the Giant commanded his wife to bring him his magic harp.

At the Giant's command, the harp, without being touched, played the most beautiful haunting music Jack had ever heard. The sweet music soon lulled the Giant to sleep and Jack, being anxious to own this wondrous instrument, came out of his hiding place, grabbed the harp and made off with it. But the magic harp called out, 'Master, Master!' and woke up the Giant who got up and chased after Jack. Jack ran as fast as he could back to the beanstalk, with the Giant in close pursuit. Jack reached it just before the Giant caught up with him. Being the more nimble, Jack soon climbed down and called out to his mother for an axe. He hacked at the beanstalk until it fell to the ground, bringing the Giant crashing down with it.

That was the end of the Giant, and from that day forward Jack and his old mother lived contentedly together, enjoying their good fortune and wanting for nothing.

Hansel and Gretel

Hansel & Gretel.

Once upon a time there lived a poor woodcutter with his wife and two children by his former marriage; a boy named Hansel and a little girl named Gretel.

One year there was a great famine in the land and the woodcutter said to his wife, 'What will become of us? How can we feed our children when we have nothing to eat ourselves?' The wife answered, 'We must take them to the forest and leave them there, or we shall all die of hunger.' Sorrowfully the woodcutter agreed to her plan.

Hansel and Gretel overheard the stepmother's words to

their father, but Hansel, thinking of a plan, slipped out of the cottage door and gathered a pocket full of pebbles that glittered and shone in the moonlight and then, returning to Gretel, he said, 'Be comforted, dear sister, God will not forsake us.'

Early next morning, the stepmother gave each child a piece of bread for their lunch, and the family set off to chop wood in the forest.

After they had walked for some time, Hansel stood still and looked back at the cottage. This he did several times until his father said, 'Hansel, what are you looking at, and why do you lag behind so?' 'Father, I am looking back at my white cat that sits on the roof and is saying goodbye to me,' said Hansel. 'You fool', said his stepmother, 'that is only the sun shining on the white chimney.' But Hansel was not really looking at his cat; each time he stopped, he dropped a white pebble on the path.

When they reached the middle of the forest, the woodcutter built a fire and said to the children, 'Rest by the fire while we go to cut wood and when we are ready I will come to fetch you.'

Hansel and Gretel waited so long that at last they fell asleep. When they awoke it was dark and they were all alone. Gretel began to weep, but Hansel said, 'Wait until the moon rises and we will quickly find our way home.' And so it was, for the moon shone on the white pebbles Hansel had dropped to show them the way. Soon they were home again and their father was very pleased to see them.

Not long after there was another famine in the land and once more they overheard their stepmother telling her husband he must leave them in the forest. This time Hansel was unable to collect any pebbles because the door had been locked, but he comforted Gretel, saying, 'God is kind and will help us.'

Next day they were given some bread to eat and the family set off for the forest again, but this time Hansel broke his bread and left a trail of crumbs as they went along.

Everything happened as before, but when the children awoke in the night, the birds had eaten the crumbs so they could not find their way back and only wandered deeper into the forest. They were lost in the forest for another day and night, with only berries to eat; they felt sure they would soon die of hunger.

Hansel & Gretel.

Then they came upon a little house made of gingerbread, with barley-sugar windows and a roof made of cake.

Hansel and Gretel were so hungry they began to nibble at pieces of the house, when suddenly the window opened and they saw a little old woman. The children were very frightened but she said, 'Ah dear children, what brought you here? Come inside, no harm will befall you.' So she took them in and gave them a meal of milk and pancakes with sugar, apples and nuts. Then she showed them two little beds into which they crept and were soon fast asleep.

Hansel and Gretel

Although the old woman had behaved kindly towards them, she was really a witch who ate children, and early in the morning while they slept, she seized Hansel and shut him in a cage. Then she woke Gretel, saying, 'Get up lazy bones; fetch water and cook some good food for your brother, for when he is fat enough, I shall eat him up.'

Poor Gretel began to cry bitterly but it was useless, for the old witch made her do as she asked.

Every morning, the old witch came to the cage and told Hansel to put out his finger so she could feel whether he was fat enough to eat. But her eyesight was bad, so she did not realize that he held out a chicken bone instead of his hand. She could not understand why he was not getting any fatter. At last she could wait no longer. 'Gretel', she called one day, 'light the oven. Be he fat or thin, this morning I will kill Hansel and eat him.'

The tears ran down Gretel's cheeks as she lit the oven, but the old witch had no pity. After a while, she said, 'Now creep in and see if the oven is hot enough.' But Gretel pretended she did not know how and asked the old witch to show her.

'You stupid goose', cried the old woman, 'I will do it myself.' As she leaned over the oven, Gretel pushed her inside and shut the door. The old witch began to howl, but Gretel left her and went to free Hansel from the cage.

Hansel sprang out and hugged and kissed his sister and they danced for joy. Having nothing more to fear from the witch, they explored her house and found chests full of gold and silver and precious jewels with which they filled their pockets.

At last, they found their way out of the forest and ran to greet their father who was overjoyed to see them. Their stepmother had died and he had not had a single happy moment since he had abandoned his children in the forest. But now their sorrows were ended. The witch's treasure made them rich and they lived together happily ever after.

The Sleeping Beauty

THE SLEEPING BEAUTY.

Once upon a time in a far-off country there lived a King and Queen who longed for a child. After many years a little girl was born to them and the King was so pleased that he ordered a great feast to be held at her christening and invited not only all their friends and relations but also the wise fairies who lived in the Kingdom.

Now there were thirteen fairies altogether but since the King and Queen had only twelve golden plates one of them, a bad fairy, was not invited.

After the feast the fairies presented the little Princess with their wonderful gifts. The first fairy gave her the gift of virtue, the second fairy gave her the gift of beauty, the third gave her riches, the fourth gave her wisdom and so on until she had everything to be desired in the world.

Just as the eleventh fairy had presented her gift to the Princess there was a great commotion and the thirteenth fairy rushed into the great hall of the Palace. She was filled with rage and envy because she had not been invited to the feast and had come to be revenged.

'In spite of the insult you have caused me I have come to present my gift to the Princess,' she cried in a wicked voice. 'Hear this—on her fifteenth birthday the Princess shall prick her finger on a spindle and fall down dead!' and she turned on her heels and was gone again.

The King and Queen were grief-stricken and a terrified silence came over the whole assembly, but the twelfth good fairy, who had not given her gift, stepped forward and said, 'I cannot stop this evil, but I can soften it for you. The Princess shall not die but will fall asleep for a hundred years.'

Time passed and the Princess grew up as good and wise and beautiful as the fairies prophesied and was loved by everyone who knew her.

On her fifteenth birthday she was wandering through the Palace when she came upon a narrow staircase she had not seen before. At the top of the staircase was a tiny door. The Princess opened the door and found an old woman sitting and spinning.

The Princess had never seen a spinning wheel because the King, to save her from the threatened evil, had commanded that all the spindles in the Kingdom should be destroyed. She asked the old woman what she was doing and reached out her hand in fascination to touch the spindle. Scarcely had she done so when the wicked fairy's prophecy was fulfilled for she pricked her finger and sank down in a deep sleep.

At the same moment, the King and the Queen and their servants slept at their work, the horses in the stable and the doves in the dovecote slept, and everything was still.

As the years passed, a thick thorny hedge grew up around the Palace hiding it from view but the story of the enchanted Palace and the beautiful sleeping Princess spread throughout the land.

A hundred years went by and it happened that a young Prince heard the legend and determined to find the Sleeping Beauty and wake her from her sleep.

It so happened that the Prince came to the Palace on the last day of the hundred years and as he approached he was amazed to see the thorny hedge turn into beautiful flowering shrubs through which he passed with ease.

As he entered the Palace he passed the King and Queen and all the courtiers and servants still slumbering peacefully. He

The Sleeping Beauty

The Sleeping Beauty.

went from room to room until he came to the tower where the Princess was sleeping. She looked so beautiful that the Prince fell in love with her immediately and stooped to kiss her. At his touch she awoke and smiled up at him and at that very moment the King and Queen and everyone in the Palace awoke and began to move and talk just as they had been doing when the enchantment fell upon them all.

Then the Prince and Princess were married with great splendour and lived together happily ever after.

Перышко Финиста Ясна-Сокола.

Once there was a Merchant who had three daughters. One day, before he set out for the Fair, he called them to him and asked, 'My daughters, what do you most desire me to buy for you at the Fair?'

The eldest answered, 'A piece of rich brocade for a gown.'

The second said, 'A fine shawl.' But the youngest replied, 'Only a scarlet flower for my window sill.'

The Merchant bade them goodbye and after some time returned with gifts for the two eldest daughters but he quite forgot the little scarlet flower, and comforted his youngest daughter saying, 'Never mind, I shall soon go again to the Fair, and this time I shall bring you a gift.

Time passed and once more the Merchant called to his three daughters saying, 'I am going to the Fair. What shall I bring for you this time?'

The eldest answered, 'Buy me a golden chain.' And the second answered, 'Buy me a pair of golden ear-rings.' But the youngest replied, 'I desire nothing but a scarlet flower to set in my window.'

Once more the Merchant returned with fine gifts for his eldest daughters but he quite forgot the scarlet flower.

Again he comforted his youngest daughter saying, 'A simple flower is no great thing. Never mind, next time I will bring you a gift.'

A third time the Merchant prepared to go to the Fair and, calling his daughters to him, he asked them what they most desired from the Fair.

The first answered, 'A pair of satin shoes.'

The second answered, 'A silken petticoat.'

But the youngest only said, 'All I desire is a scarlet flower to set in my window.'

Before returning from the Fair the Merchant purchased the satin shoes and the silken petticoat and, remembering his youngest daughter, went to look for the scarlet flower. But search as he might he could not find a single scarlet blossom in the whole town and returned home full of sadness that he must disappoint his youngest daugher for a third time.

On his journey home he met a little old man carrying a scarlet flower in a box, and catching sight of the blossom he begged and pleaded with the old man to sell it. But the old man refused saying, 'This scarlet blossom has no price—I have sworn to keep it for the maiden who is to marry my son.'

The Merchant offered everything he had for it—even the satin shoes and the silken petticoat, and at last the old man said, 'You may have the flower for your daughter but only on condition that she weds my son—Finist the Falcon.'

The Merchant considered for a moment and then replied, 'Well, old man, give me your flower and if my daughter will take your son, he shall marry her.' The old man handed him the scarlet flower and instantly disappeared and the Merchant made his way home to his daughters who were delighted to see him and receive their gifts.

He said to the youngest, 'Here is your scarlet flower, daughter, but to my sorrow I have promised that in return for it you will wed Finist the Falcon, the son of a stranger I met on the way.'

'Do not worry, Father', said the maiden, 'if Finist the Falcon will woo me, then I will wed him.'

That night she placed the little scarlet flower on the window sill of her room and was marvelling at its beauty and fragrance when suddenly through the window flew a swift beautiful falcon with brightly coloured feathers who, on entering her room, was transformed into a handsome Prince. The young Prince soothed the maiden's fright and they talked far into the night. When daybreak was near, Finist the Falcon said to her, 'Each evening when you set the scarlet flower on your window sill I will come to you; but now before I leave, take one feather from my wing and if you have need of anything wave it on your right side and you shall have whatever your heart desires.'

Each evening Finist the Falcon flew in at the window and wooed the maiden and although her elder sisters could hear voices in the night, when morning came there was never anyone in the room but their sister.

One night, determined to discover the maiden's secret, they put a sleeping powder in her drink so that she fell into a deep sleep and when Finist the Falcon came flying to the window it was locked so that although he struggled and beat against it he could not enter.

'My beautiful dearest!' he cried, 'have you stopped loving me so soon? Then I shall fly away and you must travel to the farthest shores and wear through three pairs of iron shoes before you find me again.'

But although she heard his words in her sleep, the maiden could not awaken and the Falcon flew away into the dark sky.

In the morning she saw that the window had been barred against her love and she wept bitterly. Then she thought of the bright feather and waving it on her right side she cried, 'Come to me, my own Finist the Falcon!' but he did not appear and she knew the charm was broken. Then she remembered the words

Перышко Финиста Ясна-Сокола.

she had heard in her sleep and she had three pairs of strong iron shoes made for her dainty feet and set out on her journey to find her love.

The maiden travelled for many days. She wore out the iron shoes and journeyed across many countries but still she did not find Finist the Falcon. One day, when she had almost given up hope, she met an old woman who asked her, 'Where are you going, beautiful girl?' 'Oh grandmother', she replied, 'I am searching for my dearest Finist the Falcon.'

'He is a relative of mine,' said the old woman. 'He is

staying in the Palace beside the blue ocean for he is to marry the Tsar's daughter and they are preparing for the wedding. Go now and take with you this gold and diamond ball. Perhaps you will wish to give it as a wedding gift to his bride.'

The maiden thanked the old woman and set off once more, and that afternoon she came at last to the farthest shore of the land where the blue ocean spread wide and free before her, and beside it stood a palace of white marble with golden domes that sparkled in the sunlight.

She was sitting on the soft sand tossing the gold and diamond ball in the air and wondering whether she would ever see her beloved again when the Tsar's daughter with her maids chanced to walk by. The Tsar's daughter saw the diamond ball and desired to buy it.

'You may have it', answered the maiden, 'if you will pay my price.' 'And what is your price?' asked the Tsar's daughter. 'Let me sit through the night by the side of your husband-to-be,' replied the maiden, for she knew he would be married the next day and she would never see him again. The Tsar's daughter agreed and that night after Finist the Falcon had fallen asleep she took the maiden to his room, telling her to watch over him till daybreak.

Through the long night the maiden bent over her beloved, weeping and crying, 'Finist my own dear, my bright Falcon, awake and know me. I have travelled to these far shores and worn out three pairs of iron shoes searching for you.' But Finist slept soundly and did not waken and she said to herself, 'Though he will never be mine, in the past he loved me and I shall kiss him once before I leave,' and as she leant over to kiss him her tears fell on him and woke him.

As soon as Finist the Falcon awoke he recognized the maiden and she told him how her jealous sisters had locked her window against him and how she had journeyed to find him. Finist the Falcon was so happy to find his first love back once more that he embraced her and turning into a beautiful Falcon again he set her on his coloured wings and flew away with her to his Kingdom where they were wed and lived happily ever after.

THE GOOSE GIRL.

T here was once a beautiful Princess who was betrothed to a King's son. When the time came for her to be married, it was necessary for her to travel many miles to the country where her future husband lived. Her mother was too old to travel with her, so she packed the royal bridal treasure for her and provided her with a maid to care for her on her journey, and horses for them to ride.

The horse that she gave to her daughter was called Falada and had the gift of speech.

Before the Princess departed, the Queen gave her a silken

handkerchief on which there were three drops of blood. 'Take care not to lose this handkerchief, my dear', she said, 'for it will keep you from harm!' The Princess placed the handkerchief next to her heart and bidding her mother a sorrowful farewell, mounted her horse and rode away.

After journeying for some time, they came to a stream and being hot and thirsty the Princess said to her maid, 'Please dismount and fetch me some water in that cup you carry.'

'If you are thirsty', replied the maid, 'get off your horse and fetch the water yourself. I will be your servant no longer.'

So the Princess dismounted from her horse and, lying down, she drank from the stream, holding the water in her cupped hands. When she did so she heard the handkerchief say, 'If your mother knew of this it would break her heart.'

They resumed their journey, but presently the Princess felt thirsty again and when they reached the stream she asked the maid to fetch some water, but once again the maid refused and the Princess was obliged to dismount and go to the stream herself. Again she heard the handkerchief say, 'If your mother knew of this it would break her heart,' and, as she bent over to drink, the handkerchief fell into the water and floated away without her noticing it.

The waiting maid saw what happened and was glad, because she knew the Princess would now be powerless. She said, 'Now I will ride Falada and you may ride my horse; I will wear your royal robes and you may wear my common dress.' She made the Princess promise never to reveal that she was the true Princess.

The Princess was so frightened that she promised everything the maid told her; and Falada saw and heard all that happened and remembered it.

When they arrived at the Palace the Prince came to receive the maid, believing her to be his true bride. The real Princess was left standing in the Palace yard. The old King chanced to see her there and, noticing how delicate and beautiful she was, even in her common dress, he came out to ask her name and whence she came.

She replied, 'I came all this way as a companion, but now I must find work or I shall starve.'

The King thought for a long time. 'I know a boy who looks

after the geese,' he said at last. 'He is called Conrad, you may help him.' So the real Princess went away to become a Goose girl.

Soon afterwards the false bride asked that Falada should be destroyed, for she knew the horse could speak and was afraid he would tell the Prince the truth. So poor Falada was killed and his head was placed over the gateway to the Palace. Every morning, when the geese were driven through the gateway on their way to the meadow, the Goose girl cried, 'Falada dost thou know me?' and Falada replied, 'Oh yes. You are the young Princess and if your mother knew of this it would break her heart.'

When the Goose girl and Conrad reached the meadow, she unloosened her hair of pure gold, which so enchanted the boy that he tried to touch a lock of it. But the Goose girl sang:

'Blow, blow wind. Blow Conrad's hat away.'

Immediately a strong wind took Conrad's hat and when he had chased it all over the meadow and finally retrieved it, the Goose girl had tied up her hair once more.

This happened the next day also and when they returned to the Palace that evening, Conrad told the King that he would no longer look after the geese. 'Why not?' asked the King. 'Because the Goose girl vexes me all day,' replied Conrad, and told the King of the strange things that had happened.

The King asked Conrad to take the geese as usual the next day. He waited by the gateway and heard the Goose girl speak to Falada. Then he followed them to the meadow and saw the Goose girl unloosen her hair and cause the wind to blow Conrad's hat away.

That evening the King called the Goose girl and asked her what it all meant. At last she told him she was the Princess to whom his son had been betrothed and how the wicked maid had taken her place.

On hearing her tale, the King ordered the Goose girl to be dressed in royal robes. He called the Prince to tell him how he had been tricked into taking a false bride. When he saw the beautiful Princess, the Prince immediately sent the false bride away. The true bride took her place on the throne beside him and they ruled their Kingdom in peace and happiness.

Jack the Giant Killer

Long ago in the reign of King Arthur there lived in Cornwall a worthy farmer and his son Jack. Jack was a bright and lively lad and could outwit anyone with his skill and cunning.

In those days a huge and monstrous Giant lived on St Michael's Mount off the coast of Cornwall. He was fierce and savage, the terror of all his neighbours, for he trampled their crops and stole their sheep and cattle for his larder. Jack resolved to destroy the Giant and so he took a horn, a shovel and a pickaxe to the Mount and started to dig a huge pit which he concealed with a light covering of sticks and straw. He then raised the horn to his lips and blew such a long and loud tantivy that the Giant woke with a start and ran at Jack roaring like thunder, 'You young villain! You shall pay for disturbing my rest! I shall have you for my breakfast!' And, rushing towards Jack, he fell headlong into the pit, making the whole of the Mount shake, whereupon Jack, with great daring, swiftly despatched him with a blow on the head.

Everyone rejoiced at the news of the Giant's death and the Justices of Cornwall declared that henceforth the farmer's son should be called 'Jack the Giant-Killer'.

The news of Jack's victory soon spread and another Giant, Blunderbore by name, vowed to be revenged on him.

Now this Giant lived in an enchanted castle in the middle of a lonely wood and as Jack was journeying to Wales one day he passed through the wood and being weary sat down and fell into a deep sleep. Blunderbore found him there and carried him off to his castle where he was imprisoned along with many other people in the Giant's larder. Blunderbore then went to invite another Giant to share his feast and in his absence Jack found a strong rope with which he made a noose.

As the Giants entered the castle door Jack threw the noose over their heads and pulled it tight until he had throttled them. He climbed out of the window and, taking a great bunch of keys from Blunderbore's pocket, unlocked the castle doors and liberated the Giant's captives.

Jack continued on his journey as fast as he could but night fell before he reached his destination and he sought shelter in a large house along the way which belonged to a Welsh Giant with two heads. The Welsh Giant treated Jack courteously enough but still Jack did not trust him and that night he placed a log of wood in the bed and hid himself in the corner of the room. In the middle of the night the Giant crept into the room and struck several blows on the bed where he thought Jack was sleeping.

The next morning when Jack thanked him for his hospitality the Giant asked incredulously, 'Did you sleep well? Were you not disturbed by anything in the night?' To which Jack replied, 'No, nothing but a rat that gave me three or four slaps with his tail.' The Giant wondered at this but said nothing. He gave Jack an enormous bowl of porridge for his breakfast which Jack, wishing to convince the Giant that he could eat as

much as himself, emptied into a large bag he had hidden beneath his jacket. Then, telling the Giant he would show him a little trick, he took a sharp knife and split the bag so that the porridge came out.

Not wishing to be outdone by such a little fellow, the Giant snatched up the knife and plunged it into his own stomach, and fell down dead. Thus Jack tricked the Welsh Giant and went forth on his journey.

After a few days he met with King Arthur's son who was on his way to rescue a beautiful maiden from the power of a wicked magician. The Prince was so generous and good natured that he had given away all his money to the poor and had none left for lodgings that night.

'Be of good heart!' said Jack, 'I have an uncle who lives near here. He is a huge and monstrous Giant with three heads but have no fear for I will go ahead and prepare the way.'

So Jack rode on at full speed and when he came to the door of the castle he knocked loudly. The Giant called out, 'Who dares to knock at my door?' to which Jack replied, 'It is your cousin Jack come with bad news; the King's son is coming with a thousand men to kill you and destroy all that you own!' 'Oh, cousin Jack', replied the Giant, 'I shall hide myself in the large cellar underground and you may lock me in until the King's son has gone.' This Jack did and then he fetched the Prince and they made themselves comfortable in the castle for the night while the Giant lay trembling with fear in the cellar.

The next day Jack sent the Prince on ahead while he let out his uncle, who asked Jack what he would like in return for saving his life. 'Why, good uncle', said Jack, 'I desire only the old coat and cap and the sword and slippers which hang at the end of your bed.' 'Then you shall have them', said his uncle, 'only guard them well for the coat will make you invisible, the cap will give you knowledge, the sword will cut through anything and the shoes are of great swiftness!'

Jack thanked his uncle and catching up with the Prince rode with him to the house of the bewitched maiden. She received them politely and prepared a feast for them. When they had eaten she wiped her mouth with a silken handkerchief and said to the Prince, 'Tomorrow morning you must tell me to whom I give this handkerchief or lose your head!'

The young Prince went sorrowfully to bed but Jack put on his cap of knowledge which told him that the maiden would go to meet the wicked magician and would hand him the handkerchief. So Jack put on his coat of darkness and his shoes of swiftness and followed the maiden to the middle of the forest. When she handed the handkerchief to the magician, Jack stepped forward and with his magic sword cut off his head. The maiden was immediately freed from his spell and restored to her former goodness and beauty.

Blue Beard.

The young wife turns the forbidden key
And, horror of horrors! what does she see?
The luckless victims of Bluebeard's crime,
But she herself is rescued in time.

O nce upon a time there lived a rich man who had the misfortune to have a Blue Beard which made him appear very ugly.

He wished to marry his neighbour's beautiful daughter and at length, being flattered by his attentions, she consented to be his wife, in spite of his frightful beard.

About a month after the wedding, Blue Beard was obliged to travel abroad to conduct his business, and not wishing his wife to feel lonely while he was away he gave her his bunch of keys, saying, 'Here are the keys to our great house. You may entertain your friends here in my absence; show them the magnificent rooms and the fine furniture, the gold and silver plate and the jewels I have showered on you; but on no account must you enter the small room at the end of the corridor on the ground floor.' He showed her the little key which would open the forbidden door but warned her that to use it would bring disaster upon herself.

His wife took note of all he said and for a while took great pleasure in entertaining her friends and relations but soon she began to wonder about the locked room and at last she could no longer resist the temptation to peep inside. On reaching the door she considered her husband's words of warning but curiosity overcame her and with a trembling hand she fitted the key into the lock. The door swung open immediately but it was dark in the room and it was a little while before she could see clearly. Then she perceived that the floor was covered with blood and alongside the far wall lay the bodies of several women, all of them wives that Blue Beard had married and then murdered.

She almost died with fright and in her haste to leave the place she dropped the key on the floor. She picked it up, hurriedly locked the door again and returned in horror to her bedchamber.

Noticing that the key was stained with blood she tried several times to wipe it clean, but the blood would not come off. In vain she washed and scrubbed it, and even scoured it with sand but the blood stain stayed where it was for the key was bewitched and nothing she could do would make it clean.

That evening Blue Beard returned home unexpectedly and his wife did everything in her power to convince him that she was filled with delight at his speedy return. The next morning when Blue Beard asked for the keys his wife looked so frightened that he easily guessed what had happened.

'Why is the key to my private room missing?' he asked suspiciously.

His wife was obliged to hand it to him and he immediately noticed the blood on the key. 'So, you have been into the room I forbade you to enter! Very well, since you are so fond of it, you may take your place alongside the other ladies you saw there!'

The young wife fell on her knees, weeping bitterly and begged his forgiveness for her disobedience, but Blue Beard only answered cruelly, 'You must die!' 'If I must die', cried his wife, 'at least allow me some time to say a prayer.' 'I will give you half of a quarter of an hour', replied the cruel Blue Beard, 'and not a moment more.'

His wife ran to find her sister and cried, 'Sister Anne, I beg you, run up to the tower and see if my brothers are coming to visit me, and if you see them, beckon them to make haste.'

Sister Anne ran to the top of the tower to keep watch and every few minutes the agitated wife cried out, 'Do you see anyone coming yet?' But there was no one in sight.

Finally Blue Beard shouted in a great rage, 'Wife, come down at once or I shall come to get you!'

His wife called softly for the last time, 'Sister Anne, are my brothers coming yet?' And this time her sister replied, ' I see two men on horseback but they are still at a great distance; I will give them a sign.' At that moment Blue Beard roared so loudly for his wife that the whole house shook and she dared not delay any longer.

She threw herself at his feet and once more begged him to spare her life but to no avail for he seized his scimitar and prepared to cut off her head.

At that moment the door burst open and in rode the two brothers. They drew their swords and rushed furiously at Blue Beard who tried to save himself by running away. But they seized him before he had taken twenty steps and plunged their swords into his body whereupon he fell dead at their feet. The poor wife sank to the ground in shock and relief and upon her recovery she found herself the possessor of her dead husband's great fortune for he had no heir. She used her riches to secure captains' commissions in the army for the two brothers who saved her life and gave a huge marriage dowry to her sister Anne, and soon after she herself remarried a kind and worthy gentleman who loved her and cherished her and made her forget Blue Beard's cruelty.

FROG:PRINCE......

Once upon a time, in a country far away, there was a handsome young Prince who had the misfortune to offend a wicked fairy. In order to avenge herself, the fairy had cast a spell over the Prince, turning him into an ugly frog and casting him into a deep well to live.

The King of the neighbouring country had a daughter who was so beautiful that even the sun was enchanted every time he saw her. On fine days when the sun shone warmly the Princess sometimes came to the Palace courtyard to amuse herself by tossing a golden ball high into the air and catching it as it fell.

The Frog Prince

In the middle of the courtyard was the very well in which lived the enchanted Frog Prince. He watched the Princess running to and fro in the sunshine and thought she was the prettiest creature he had ever seen.

One day it happened that the Princess could not catch her golden ball and it bounced on the stones and fell with a splash into the water.

She ran down to the edge of the well and gazed down; but the golden ball had sunk far, far out of sight, and only a little ring of bubbles showed her where it had disappeared. She began to cry bitterly.

As she wept, a voice called out, 'Don't cry, Princess!' and looking up she saw an ugly frog stretching its head out of the water.

'What will you give me if I bring your ball back from the bottom of the well?' he croaked.

'Oh, I will give you anything I have, dear frog', replied the Princess. 'My pretty dress, my diamonds; even the crown on my head. Only bring my ball back to me.'

'I do not want your dress or your diamonds or your crown', said the frog, 'but if you will promise to love me and let me be your playmate, to eat out of your plate, drink out of your cup and sleep in your silken bed, I will bring back your ball safely.'

The Princess promised, for she thought to herself, 'What a silly frog. He could never get out of that well and walk all the way to the Palace! He will never find me!' The frog dived to the bottom of the well and soon returned with the ball.

The Princess had no sooner snatched the ball from the frog than she forgot all about her promise and ran back to the Palace laughing with joy.

The next day, as she sat at dinner with the King and his courtiers, something came flopping up the great staircase—flip, flap, flop!—and a voice said:

> From the deep and mossy well,
> Little playmate where I dwell,
> When you wept in grief and pain
> I brought your golden ball again.

The Princess dropped her spoon with a clatter on to her plate, for she knew it was the frog come to claim her promise.

'What is the matter daughter?' asked the King. 'There is

someone knocking at the door; your rosy cheeks are quite pale.'

The Princess had to tell her father how she had dropped the golden ball into the well, and how the frog had brought it up for her, and of all the promises she had made to him.

Then the King frowned and said, 'People who make promises must keep them. Open the door and let the frog enter.'

The Princess opened the door unwillingly, and the frog hopped into the room, looking up into her face with his ugly popping eyes.

'Lift me up beside you', he croaked, 'that I may eat out of your plate and drink out of your cup.' The Princess did as he asked her, and was obliged to finish her own dinner with the frog beside her, for the King sat by to see that she fulfilled her promise.

When they had finished, the frog hopped down from his chair and croaked, 'I have had enough to eat and now I am tired. Take me up and lay me down on your silken pillow, that I may go to sleep.'

The Princess began to cry. It was so dreadful to think that an ugly frog, all cold and damp from the well, should sleep on her pretty white bed. But her father frowned again and said, 'People who make promises must keep them. He gave you back your golden ball and so you must do as he asks.'

So the Princess picked up the frog between her thumb and forefinger, not touching him more than she could help, carried him upstairs and put him in a corner of her room. Then she jumped into bed, meaning to leave him there, but he hopped up to her and said, 'Little playmate, I am so tired and I want to go to sleep. Lay me on your pillow or I will tell your father.'

Then the Princess was very angry; she picked him up and flung him with all her might against the wall, crying, 'Sleep there you dreadful ugly frog.'

But as he fell he was changed from an ugly frog back into the handsome young Prince and he cried, 'Oh, Princess, you have broken the wicked fairy's spell and I am myself again. Now you shall be my wife, for you are the prettiest Princess in the world and I have loved you from the first moment I saw you!'

The Princess took him to her father and the ugly frog became her husband and they lived happily ever after.

The Three Bears

Somebody's been sitting on my chair!

Once upon a time there were three Bears who lived in a little wooden house in the middle of the forest. There was a Father Bear, a Mother Bear and a tiny Baby Bear.

Every morning Mother Bear made them all porridge for breakfast, but one morning it was too hot to eat so they decided to take a walk in the forest while it cooled.

No sooner had they left the house than a little girl named Goldilocks, came skipping through the trees. She was an inquisitive child and when she came upon the little house she was determined to find out who lived there. She knocked at the door and when there was no answer she lifted the latch and crept inside.

She saw Father Bear's great big chair and tried sitting on it, but it was too big and too hard for her. Then she saw Mother Bear's middle-sized chair and tried sitting on that but it was too soft for her. Then she saw Baby Bear's little chair and tried sitting on that. It was just the right size for her and very comfortable but she sat so heavily on it that it broke into pieces. Then she noticed the three bowls of porridge on the table.

First she tasted Father Bear's porridge but it was much too hot and salty. Then she tasted Mother Bear's porridge but that

The Three Bears

Somebody's been eating my porridge!

was cold and much too sweet. Last of all she tasted Baby Bear's porridge and that was just right so she ate it all up.

After eating the porridge Goldilocks felt sleepy so she went up the stairs into the bedroom to lie down. First she lay on Father Bear's great big bed but it was so hard and lumpy that she jumped off quickly. Then she tried Mother Bear's middle-sized bed but that was too soft and had too many pillows.

Then she tried Baby Bear's bed. The little bed was just the right size and so cosy that she fell fast asleep and did not hear when the three Bears returned from their walk. The Bears noticed immediately that someone had been in their house.

'Someone has been sitting in my chair,' growled Father Bear in his great big voice.

'And someone has been sitting in my chair,' cried Mother Bear in her middle-sized voice.

'And someone has been sitting in my chair', wailed Baby Bear in his little wee voice, 'and they have broken it all up!'

Then they looked at the bowls of porridge on the table.

'Someone has been tasting my porridge,' growled Father Bear in his great big voice.

The Three Bears

There she goes!

'And someone has been tasting my porridge,' cried Mother Bear in her middle-sized voice.

'And someone has been tasting my porridge', wailed Baby Bear in his little wee voice, 'and they have eaten it all up!'

The three Bears were very cross and decided to search the house to see if the intruder was still there.

Up the stairs they went. Father Bear followed by Mother Bear and little Baby Bear scrambled along behind.

'Someone has been lying on my bed,' growled Father Bear in his great big voice.

'And someone has been lying on my bed,' cried mother Bear in her middle-sized voice when she found her pillows scattered on the floor.

'And someone has been lying on my bed', wailed Baby Bear in his little wee voice, 'and she's still here!'

All this commotion woke Goldilocks who had a great fright when she saw the three Bears standing over her. She jumped out of the bed and ran down the stairs and out of the house as fast as her legs could carry her, and she did not stop running until she was safe home again.

Dick Whittington

Dick Whittington

Long ago there lived a poor boy called Dick Whittington. His mother and father died when he was very young, and he had no one to care for him. His clothes were poor and ragged and he was often hungry. He had heard people speak of the great city of London where people were rich and the streets were paved with gold and, although it was many miles to London from the village where he lived, Dick tied his few belongings in a bundle and set off to seek his fortune.

When he reached the great city, Dick was amazed at the sight of so many fine buildings, and even more surprised to see how many people lived there and to hear how noisy it was. He soon found that work and money were no easier to find in the city than in the countryside and, search as he might, he could not find the streets paved with gold. As night fell he grew tired and hungry and, having nowhere else to go, he curled up in the nearest doorway to rest.

The doorway was the entrance to a fine house belonging to a rich merchant called Mr Fitzwarren. He was a kindly gentleman and when he arrived home to find Dick asleep on his doorstep he spoke gently to him and helped him inside. He listened to Dick's story, and when he had finished he said, 'I cannot promise that you will find your fortune, but you may work in my house, and you will have food enough to eat and a roof over your head.' And he sent his cook to prepare some food for Dick and to find him some clothes to wear.

The cook, however, did not take kindly to Dick, and scolded him often and made him work very hard for his keep. Mr Fitzwarren's daughter, Alice, took pity on Dick and ordered the cook to treat him more kindly.

A bed was made up for him in the attic but he slept very little, being greatly disturbed by the rats and mice that shared his room and ran over his head at night, and he wished he had a cat to chase them away. The next day he went to the market and with his last penny bought a cat, who quickly chased all the mice from his room, and soon became his great friend.

One day Mr Fitzwarren called his servants and told them that one of his trading ships was about to set sail for foreign parts, and asked them whether they had any goods they wished to send with it to sell. Only Dick had nothing to send—for he owned nothing in the world but his cat, and he did not wish to lose her. But at length he was persuaded to let her go, to see whether she could make his fortune.

He was sad and lonely without her, and furthermore, in spite of Miss Alice's warning, the cook became more cruel to poor Dick, so that early one morning he decided to run away. As he walked through the streets of London he heard the sound of bells from the church at Bow; they seemed to be saying:

'Turn again Whittington, Lord Mayor of London,
Turn again Whittington, Thrice Mayor of London.

At their bidding Dick turned back, crept into bed before anyone missed him, and thought on what the bells had told him.

Meanwhile, Mr Fitzwarren's ship had anchored in a foreign port and the Captain went to the King's Palace to trade with him. The King and the Captain sat down to discuss their business over a sumptuous meal as was the custom in those parts, but before they had even started to eat, hordes of rats rushed in and devoured the food. This amazed the Captain, who could not understand why the King did not keep a cat in the Palace to rid them of the rats.

Dick Whittington

'A cat? What is a cat?' Asked the King, who had never seen such a creature, and he offered great riches to the Captain if he could bring one to the Palace.

The Captain returned to his ship and fetched Dick's cat. He led her back to the Palace, and she made short work of the rats and mice!

The King was delighted and gave the Captain a casket of gold and precious jewels in exchange for the cat, and bought all the other goods on board the ship as well.

A few days later the ship set sail for England once more and the Captain was pleased to tell Mr Fitzwarren the good news of his successful voyage. When he learned of the fortune the King had paid for Dick's cat, Mr Fitzwarren sent for Dick and said, 'Now you are a very rich man, Mr Whittington. Your cat has made your fortune!'

Dick was very happy to hear the news, for now that he was a rich man he felt able to tell Mr Fitzwarren that he had fallen in love with his daughter, Alice, and to ask for her hand in marriage.

Mr Fitzwarren was happy to give his consent to the wedding, for he was fond of Dick, and in due course they were married, and Dick entered into a partnership with his father-in-law.

Dick Whittington's good fortune did not make him proud or overbearing; he was loved and admired by all who knew him, and became well known for his charity towards the poor and needy.

He was eventually made Lord Mayor of London, an office that he filled with such prudence and distinction that the honour was bestowed on him twice more—thus fulfilling the promise told to him by the Bow Bells:

'Turn again Whittington, Lord Mayor of London,
Turn again Whittington, thrice Mayor of London.'

Tom Thumb

O nce upon a time there lived a poor peasant and his wife, who were very sad because they had no children. 'Oh,' sighed the wife, 'if we had but one child and he were no bigger than my thumb I should be content and love him with all my heart.'

It so happened that soon afterwards they had a son who, although perfectly formed, was actually no bigger than a thumb. So they remarked to one another that it had happened just as they had wished; and they called the child Tom Thumb.

He was a clever and merry child but, though his parents

gave him the most nourishing food, he never grew an inch. One day when his father was going out to gather wood, Tom Thumb begged to be allowed to drive the horse and cart.

'You!', cried his father, 'why you are no bigger than my thumb! You are much too small to lead the horse by the bridle.'

'Ah, but put me on the horse's ear', said Tom Thumb, 'then go ahead and gather the wood and I will follow.' He pleaded so hard that at last his father agreed and put him on the horse's ear and told him how to guide it. 'Gee up,' shouted the little man into the ear and the horse started immediately.

As he went along the road he met two strange men who were so astonished to see a cart and horse without a driver that they turned round and followed it into the forest.

When Tom saw his father he called out, 'Look father, how well I have driven! Now please lift me down again!' His father set him safely on the ground where he sat comfortably on a thistle. The two strangers gazed at him in astonishment and one of them whispered, 'What a lot of money we could make if we had that funny little fellow to exhibit in the town,' and they went to the father and said, 'We would like to buy this funny little creature, if you are willing to sell him.'

'Oh no', replied the old peasant, 'he is my son, and poor as I am, I would not sell him for all the money in the world.'

But Tom Thumb crept upon his father's shoulders and whispered in his ear, 'Sell me to these men, I am sure they will treat me well and I will come back very soon.'

So the strangers gave the peasant a large sum of money and took Tom Thumb away with them. One of the men put him on the brim of his hat, where he travelled very comfortably. When evening came he asked the man to lift him down and no sooner was he on the ground than he ran away as fast as his legs could carry him. He found an empty snail shell in which he hid until the men gave up the search for him and went home.

After a while Tom heard other voices. 'There is plenty of gold in the Rector's house', said one, 'if only we could get in.'

'I will help you,' shouted Tom from the snail shell. The thieves were astounded to hear a voice at their feet and even more so when they saw the tiny fellow from which it came.

'Take me with you,' said Tom. 'I can creep through the tiniest window and hand out whatever you want.'

The thieves agreed and they all set off for the Rectory. When they arrived the men lifted Tom through the window and when he was safely inside he called out in a loud voice, 'What do you want me to steal first?'

'Not so loud,' said the thieves in a great fright. 'You will wake the whole house.'

Tom Thumb, pretending he could not hear shouted louder than ever. 'Shall I hand you the gold and silver?' and went on making such a noise that he woke the servants, and the thieves ran away in terror.

Tom slipped out of the window so quickly that no one saw him and crept into a barn where he made a comfortable bed in the hay and was soon fast asleep.

Early next morning the servant came to feed the cow, and took an armful of the hay in which Tom was sleeping. Tom was so tired that he did not wake until he found himself in the cow's mouth. He had to jump about to avoid her teeth and was quite relieved when she swallowed him.

'Now I am really done for!' he thought. It was dreadfully dark inside the cow and she was eating such large quantities of hay that soon there was scarcely room to move.

Tom Thumb began to call out in terror, as loudly as he could. 'No more hay! no more hay!'

When the milkmaid heard the voice she was so frightened that she upset the milk pail and ran to tell her master that the cow had spoken.

'Nonsense', said the Rector, but he came out to the barn and heard Tom calling out, 'No more hay, no more hay.' 'This cow is possessed by an evil spirit,' said the Rector and ordered it to be killed at once.

No sooner was the animal cut up than Tom popped out and ran away as fast as his legs would carry him; and never stopped until he reached his home.

His father and mother were so overjoyed to see him safe and sound that they kissed him a hundred times and vowed that they would not sell him again for all the gold in the world.

Cinderella

Cinderella.

Once upon a time there was a man whose wife had died, leaving him to care for their little daughter. Soon afterwards the father took a second wife but she had two daughters of her own and cared nothing for her stepdaughter and treated her cruelly, making her cook and work all day.

The maiden was dressed in ragged old clothes and slept by the fire among the cinders, so they called her Cinderella.

One day the King gave a grand ball to which he invited all the young ladies in the land, so that his son, the Prince, might choose a bride. The two stepsisters were overjoyed to receive an

invitation and ordered Cinderella to make ready their finest clothes and dress their hair so that they could look their best at the King's palace.

Cinderella longed to go to the ball too but when she asked her stepsisters they laughed and said, 'You, Cinderella? You are all dirty and have no fine dresses, how can you go to the ball!'

When her stepsisters had left for the palace, Cinderella sat down and wept bitterly at her misfortune.

Suddenly her fairy Godmother appeared and asked poor Cinderella what ailed her.

Cinderella

CINDERELLA

'Oh, how I wish I could go to the ball,' cried Cinderella. 'Hush, my child,' said the kind fairy Godmother. 'You shall go to the ball. Find me a pumpkin and fetch the mouse trap.'

Cinderella brought the finest pumpkin she had and at the touch of the fairy Godmother's wand it became a fine gilded coach. She rescued the white mice from the trap and the fairy Godmother turned them into six white horses to pull the coach.

'And now, my child, you must have a fine gown to wear to the ball,' and she waved her wand over Cinderella. The rags she wore became a beautiful ball gown encrusted with precious jewels and on her feet she wore a pair of delicate glass slippers.

Before she went, the fairy Godmother warned Cinderella she must leave the ball before the clock struck midnight for if she stayed a moment longer her coach and horses would disappear and her fine clothes would become rags again.

Cinderella looked so beautiful when she entered the ballroom that her stepsisters did not recognize her. The Prince was enchanted by her and they danced together the whole evening. The time passed so quickly that Cinderella quite forgot her fairy Godmother's warning, when suddenly she heard the clock begin to strike twelve o'clock.

She ran out of the ballroom as fast as her feet would carry her, and in her haste dropped one of the glass slippers. Cinderella arrived home tired and breathless in her ragged clothes and without her coach and horses and went to sleep in her usual place by the fire.

Meanwhile the Prince searched for the beautiful maiden with whom he had fallen in love but found only the glass slipper she had left behind. A few days later it was proclaimed that the Prince would marry the maiden whose foot exactly fitted the slipper he had found. Accordingly his messengers took the slipper to each of the ladies who had attended the ball but none could fit it on.

Both the stepsisters tried without success and the Prince's servant then asked the father, 'Have you no other daughter whom the shoe might fit?'

'Only the daughter of my first wife', he replied, 'but she is a poor little Cinderella not fit to be a Prince's wife.' The servant insisted she be sent for and made her put on the slipper, which was found to fit exactly.

Then she raised her head and looked up at the Prince who immediately recognized the beautiful maiden with whom he had danced at the ball and exclaimed, 'This is my bride!'

So they were married and lived in peace and happiness ever after.

The Yellow Dwarf.

The Yellow Dwarf was a doubtful friend
He caused two lovers untimely end,
And from their graves, in wind and weather,
Two fair trees grew and mingled together.

There was once a Princess who was so beautiful she was called All-Fair, but being only too well aware of her own beauty, she grew up vain and proud and spoilt.

Her portrait was painted by the best artists, the most renowned poets in the land penned verses to her beauty and twenty kings were her suitors. Her mother, the Queen, encouraged her to believe she was the most beautiful, the most charming, the most desirable creature in the world and was overjoyed by the adoration of her suitors. However, when All-Fair declared that none of them was worthy enough to deserve her hand in marriage, the Queen began to despair, thinking that her daughter would die an old maid in spite of her beauty, and scolded her for her cruelty and indifference towards them all, but All-Fair merely tossed her head and stuck her nose in the air.

At length, being at her wits' end, the Queen went to seek the advice of a wise Fairy. The Fairy was guarded by two lions, who would allow a stranger to approach only if they were presented with a cake made from millet, sugar candy and crocodiles' eggs.

The Queen prepared a cake and carried it with her in a little basket. After walking some distance she stopped to rest in the shade of an orange tree and fell fast asleep.

On waking she found both the basket and the cake were missing, and to her horror heard the growls of the lions in the distance. 'Alas', she cried, 'what will become of me and who will care for my dear daughter?' She wept bitterly at her misfortune, when suddenly she heard a voice calling her and, looking up, she saw a little man in the tree.

The Yellow Dwarf—for it was he—said, 'Oh, Queen, I know you and the trouble you are in. If you will promise me your daughter for my wife I will save you from the lions.'

In her fear and distress the Queen cried, 'Good Sir Dwarf, All-Fair is yours.' And at her words the orange tree opened and the Queen hid inside and escaped from the lions.

She came out of the tree to find herself in a field full of thistles and nettles and surrounded by a muddy ditch. In the middle of the field stood a mean little thatched house. The Yellow Dwarf came out of the door and approached the Queen, saying, 'Good Mother-in-law, this is the house where your daughter will live with me; she will have an ass to ride through the nettles and thistles, and water to drink from the stream, and the frogs that are fattened in it will be her food. She will not want for anything and I will never leave her.'

The Queen was horrified when she realized what she had done, and fell into a fit of melancholy which dismayed her daughter so much that she too resolved to visit the wise Fairy to seek her advice. She took a cake of millet, sugar candy and crocodiles' eggs to appease the guardian lions and set off on the journey.

When she reached the orange tree she sat down to rest and

fell fast asleep. When she awoke the cake had vanished and she wept bitterly, knowing she could never pass the lions and speak with the Fairy. Just then the Yellow Dwarf appeared, and told All-Fair how the Queen had promised him her daughter's hand in marriage. All-Fair was filled with horror at his words, and fell into a swoon, and when she recovered she was back in her own bed.

Remembering all that had passed, All-Fair became as melancholy as her mother, and finally she decided that she would marry the most powerful of the twenty kings; the one who could protect her from the Yellow Dwarf. To this end she chose the King of the Golden Mines—a strong and handsome man who loved her passionately. In time All-Fair began to love him in return, and at last the marriage was arranged and the ceremony was proclaimed with bells and trumpets.

As the King and All-Fair left the Palace they were confronted by an ugly old woman. It was the wise Fairy come to avenge her friend, the Yellow Dwarf. She was closely followed by the Dwarf himself, mounted on the back of a large cat. The Yellow Dwarf sprang at the King, who drew his cutlass to defend himself and his new bride, but suddenly a mist came over his eyes and he found himself lifted up and carried away by the Fairy, who imprisoned him in a cave near the sea shore.

One day, having flattered the Fairy with soft words, the King persuaded her to allow him to take a walk along the sea shore.

As he walked he heard a voice calling him and, looking round, he saw a mermaid, who said to him, 'I know how sad you are to be parted from your bride. If you wish I will take you away from this place to the Castle where the Yellow Dwarf holds her prisoner.' And she set the King upon her fish's tail and swam away to the Yellow Dwarf's Castle.

'Here you will find your Princess', said the mermaid, 'but you must face many enemies before you come to her. Take this sword and never let it out of your hand, for it will protect you and help you face the greatest dangers.'

After these words the mermaid gave him the sword, which was made from an entire diamond and shone as brightly as the sun itself.

The King thanked the mermaid warmly and desired her to

grant him her protection as he went to rescue his beloved Princess.

As the King advanced towards the Castle he was set upon by four terrible sphinxes who would have torn him into a thousand pieces had it not been for the mermaid's sword which glittered so in their eyes that they were blinded and fell at his feet.

Then he met six dragons with scaly skins as hard as iron, but the mermaid's sword cut them to pieces with ease.

Next he came to four-and-twenty maidens who guarded the Castle. He knew he would have to kill the fair maidens to reach his beloved and faltered in his task. But then he heard a voice cry, 'Strike, strike, or you will lose your Princess for ever,' and he threw himself into their midst and soon dispersed them, whereupon he came to his beloved All-Fair and threw himself at her feet, letting the sword fall from his grasp.

No sooner had he dropped the sword than the Yellow Dwarf appeared from his hiding place and ran to seize it.

'Now', said the Dwarf, brandishing the sword, 'I am master of your fate. I will grant you your life and liberty on condition that you consent to my marriage with the Princess.'

'I will die a thousand deaths before I do such a thing,' cried the brave King.

'Alas, that thought is the most terrible of all,' sobbed the Princess. 'I would sooner consent to marry the Dwarf.'

'If you marry him my life will be worth nothing,' interrupted the King. 'It shall not be.'

'No, it shall not be', replied the Dwarf, 'for a beloved rival I cannot bear.' At these words he stabbed the King to the heart.

The Princess, being unable to live without him, fell to the ground in a swoon and died of a broken heart.

The kindly mermaid was powerless to save the unfortunate lovers, but as a tribute to their love she changed them into two palm trees which grew entwined together beside the shore.

Snow White

SNOWDROP.

Long ago, in the middle of winter, a Queen sat sewing at an ebony-framed window looking out at the snow. Suddenly she pricked her finger and a drop of blood fell on to the snow. As she looked at it she said to herself, 'Oh, if only I had a child with skin as white as snow, lips as red as blood and hair as black as ebony.'

Soon afterwards she had a beautiful baby daughter just as she had wished and she called her Snow White.

But the Queen died and a year later the King took another wife. She was a beautiful woman, but proud and vain and could not bear anyone to be prettier than herself. She possessed a magic mirror and every day she looked into it and asked,

> Mirror, Mirror on the wall,
> Who is fairest of them all?

and every day the mirror replied,

> Queen though art fairest of them all.

On the day of Snow White's seventh birthday, the Queen asked her mirror the usual question, but this time the mirror replied,

> Queen, thou art most fair to see,
> But Snow White fairer still will be.

At this the Queen turned green with jealousy and she began to hate her stepdaughter.

One day she told her huntsman to take the child to the forest and kill her. The huntsman led Snow White to the forest but could not bear to hurt her, so he told her to run far away and hide.

Snow White ran and ran until she came upon a tiny cottage. Inside there was a little table laid with plates and mugs for seven people and against the wall there were seven little beds. Snow White was so tired that she lay down on one of the beds and fell fast asleep.

Although Snow White did not know, the cottage belonged to seven dwarfs who mined gold in the mountains. They were astonished to discover Snow White when they returned from their day's work, but they were very kind hearted and when they heard her story they asked her to stay with them.

So Snow White took care of the little cottage each day when the dwarfs went off to work, and each day they warned her, 'Beware of your stepmother. Do not let anyone enter the cottage.' All this time the wicked Queen imagined Snow White was dead, but one day she went to her mirror again and asked,

> Mirror, Mirror on the wall,
> Who is fairest of them all?

and the mirror answered,

> Oh Queen, thou art most fair to see,
> But Snow White is still more fair than thee.

And the Queen knew the huntsman had deceived her and once again jealousy raged within her. She made plans to get rid of Snow White. She disguised herself as an old pedlar woman and

Christmas Wishes.   Little Snow White.

went in search of the dwarfs' cottage. When she found it she called out, 'Fine goods to sell, fine ribbons and lace.'

Snow White thought the old woman looked so harmless that she opened the door to her and bought lace and ribbons. Then the old woman said, 'Come my dear, I will show you how to lace your bodice.' But she laced poor Snow White's bodice so tightly that she could not breathe and sank to the floor as though dead.

'Now I shall be the most beautiful', said the Queen and she went straight home and asked the mirror,

Snow White

Mirror, Mirror on the wall,
Who is the fairest of them all?
and was greatly surprised when the mirror replied,
Oh Queen thou art most fair to see
But Snow White is still more fair than thee.

For soon after the wicked Queen had left the cottage the dwarfs had returned home and finding Snow White unconscious had unlaced her bodice and quickly revived her.

When she realized this the Queen was more furious than ever and set about finding another way to kill Snow White.

She poisoned a rosy apple and returned to the dwarfs' cottage disguised as a farmer's wife. When the Queen knocked at the cottage door, Snow White looked out of the window and said, 'The dwarfs have forbidden me to open the door to anyone for fear of my stepmother.'

'Do not be afraid, I am only a farmer's wife come to give you this rosy apple,' said the Queen. 'Here I will hand it through the window.' The apple looked so tempting that Snow White accepted it, but as soon as she took a bite, she fell to the ground dead. This time the Queen was sure her plan had worked and was delighted when the mirror replied to her usual question.

Queen of Beauty shalt thou be
There is none as fair as thee.

When the dwarfs returned home that night and found Snow White they wept and mourned but could not restore her to life. So they made a beautiful glass coffin and laid her in it and carried her up into the mountains where the birds could watch over her.

One day a handsome Prince came riding by and saw Snow White lying in the glass coffin. She looked so beautiful that he fell deeply in love and would not leave her side. The dwarfs were so full of pity for him when they heard this that they allowed the Prince to take Snow White away with him, but as his servants carried the coffin down the mountain, one stumbled and the jolt dislodged the piece of apple from Snow White's mouth and she came to life again.

The Prince was overjoyed and asked Snow White to be his wife. They were married with great pomp and ceremony and Snow White was more beautiful than ever as a bride.

List of Illustrators